James
and the
Dinosaurs

by Doug Johnson
illustrated by Bill Basso

ATHENEUM BOOKS FOR YOUNG READERS

Atheneum Books for Young Readers
An imprint of Simon & Schuster Children's Publishing Division
1230 Avenue of the Americas
New York, NY 10020

The text of this book is set in Cooper Bold.
The illustrations were done in watercolor.
Designed by Angela Carlino

First edition
Printed in the United States of America

10 9 8 7 6 5 4 3 2 1

Library of Congress Cataloging-in-Publication Data
Johnson, Doug, 1949-
James and the dinosaurs / by Doug Johnson ; illustrated by Bill Basso. — 1st ed.
p.   cm.
Summary: When his teacher tells him that he will not have to do his classwork if he can find a dinosaur,
James is determined to find one and bring it to school.
ISBN 0-689-31965-7 :
[1. Dinosaurs—Ficton.] I. Basso, Bill, ill. II. Title.
pZ7.J631715Jam   1995
[E]—dc20
95-5275
CIP
AC

To children everywhere: Hold on to your dreams
—D. J.

For Marie, Billy, James, and Marie Louise
—B. B.

It was Friday, and James hadn't done his classwork all week.

All James did was talk about dinosaurs and draw pictures of them. He drew dinosaurs in his notebook instead of doing his work. During recess he drew dinosaurs in the playground. He even had dreams about baseball-playing dinosaurs. They seemed so real!

Mr. Gordon liked James, but finally he had enough. The class giggled as he wrote James a note on the blackboard. But James just smiled.

James worked at his desk during recess. Mr. Gordon stopped by James's desk and peered over his shoulder.

"James, what are you doing? That isn't your classwork."

James smiled. "I've made a list."

"A list of what?" asked Mr. Gordon.

"A list of all the places I might find a dinosaur."

Mr. Gordon chuckled. "Your classwork now, please. Do you understand?"

James sighed. "Yes, Mr. Gordon."

But James left school that day feeling very determined. Maybe if I can bring Mr. Gordon a whole bunch of dinosaurs, James thought, I'll never have to do classwork again!

That night James happily went to sleep with dinosaur dreams filling his head.

James ate a quick breakfast Saturday morning and headed to the first place on his list—the playground. He looked for dinosaurs as soon as he got there. He looked at the kids riding on the swings. No dinosaurs. He made a circle around the teeter-totter. No dinosaurs. He watched the kids hanging from the monkey bars. No dinosaurs.

James checked his list. Of course! They're at the shopping mall! he thought confidently. James sped past the slide on his way out of the playground.

James wandered around the shopping mall. He looked in all the stores. No dinosaurs. He searched the food court. No dinosaurs. James walked past the escalator, reading his list.

"Maybe they're at the fall festival parade," he said, feeling just a little worried. He was out of the mall in a flash.

At the parade, James watched the marching bands. No dinosaurs. He watched the clowns. No dinosaurs. James was discouraged. He walked down the street as the crowd cheered the beauty queen.

James sighed and looked over his list. They've got to be at the carnival, he thought, and he trudged over to the fairgrounds.

James watched the people playing games at the carnival. No dinosaurs. He looked up at the people screaming and laughing on the rides. No dinosaurs. Where could they be? James wondered in frustration. He kicked an empty soda can.

But a few minutes later, a grin began to creep across James's face. "Maybe I've been wrong. Maybe they don't like being around a lot of people," he said to himself. James raced past the merry-go-round and out of the fairgrounds.

James picked his way among the broken-down cars in the junkyard.
No dinosaurs. He went around the forklift. No dinosaurs. James heard the
crunch of the car crusher. He didn't even turn around and watch. He
couldn't believe he hadn't found any dinosaurs.

James thought of all the places he'd been as he lay in bed that night. Maybe I didn't look hard enough, James thought sadly as he drifted off to sleep. He dreamed about baseball-playing dinosaurs all night long.

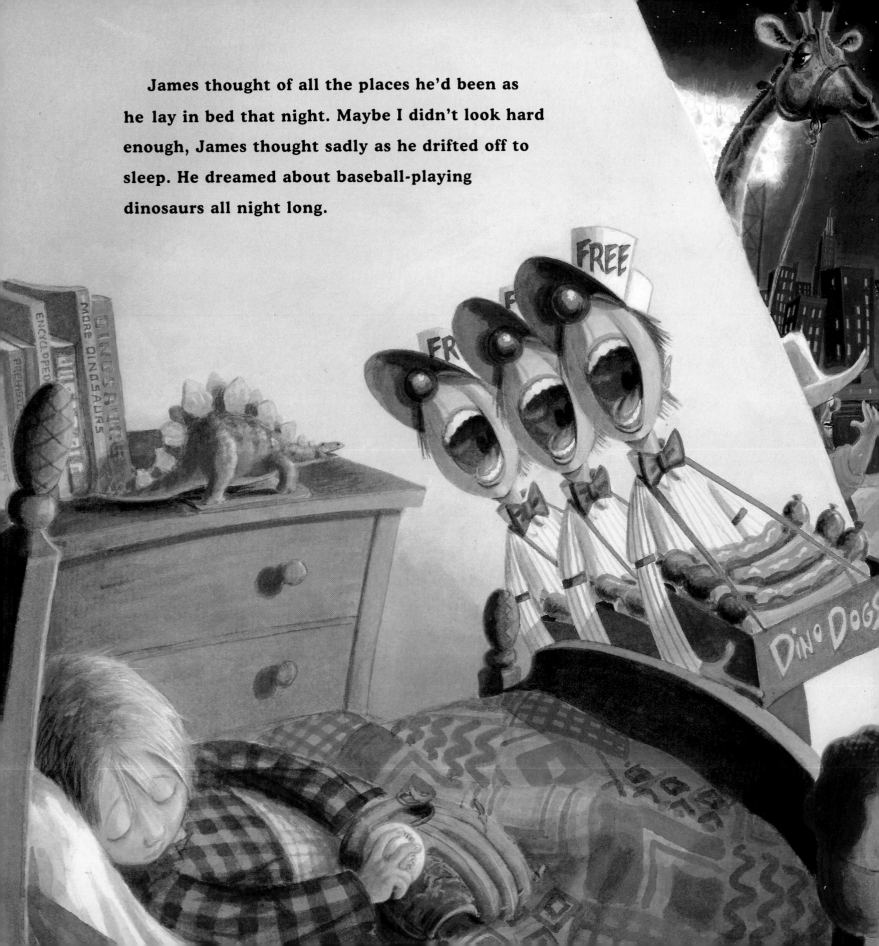

James shook himself when he woke up Sunday morning. "That dream sure seemed real! There must be dinosaurs somewhere!" he said out loud. James went to the backyard. He poked around his mother's garden. No dinosaurs. He looked inside his father's workshop. No dinosaurs.

James got so upset he threw a baseball into the woods behind his house. He didn't bother to look where it landed.

That day James did all his overdue classwork. On Monday he would be ready for Mr. Gordon.

But as he walked to school the next day, James just had to look one more time. He looked in front of him. No dinosaurs. He looked to the left of him. No dinosaurs. He looked to the right of him. No dinosaurs.

"It's hopeless! There aren't any dinosaurs anywhere," he muttered to himself.

James walked up to the front of the classroom. "Here's my work, Mr. Gordon."

Mr. Gordon smiled. "Thank you, James. I can see you've worked very hard. And I've been thinking about something. Your classwork is important, but you also know a lot about dinosaurs. How would you like to tell the class about them?"

"Oh Mr. Gordon, that would be neat!"

"Then meet me tomorrow morning at 8:15, and we'll make some plans."

James came to school early the next morning. He found Mr. Gordon in the hallway staring at the floor. Large, strange-looking footprints led right to their classroom door. James looked up at Mr. Gordon. Mr. Gordon just scratched his head. He looked at James. He scratched his head again. But he didn't say anything.

For the rest of the year, James did his classwork. He didn't mind.

Maybe, just maybe...